LEGO KNIGHTS' KINGDOM™

The Dark Fortress

by Daniel Lipkowitz

Illustrated by Mada Design, Inc.

SCHOLASTIC INC.

New York   Toronto   London   Auckland   Sydney

Mexico City   New Delhi   Hong Kong   Buenos Aires

ISBN 0-439-74568-3

12 11 10 9 8 7 6 5 4 3   5 6 7 8 9/0

Designed by Rick DeMonico

Printed in the U.S.A.
First printing, October 2005

Prologue
A Villain Returns

The dark knight Vladek sat alone in his prison cell, but he did not intend to stay there for long. He would have his revenge on the four knights who had defeated him.

When the guards next checked the cell, it was empty. Vladek had escaped!

Chapter 1
A Dangerous Mission

"The Book of Morcia has terrible news," said King Mathias to his four bravest knights. "One of our castles has been attacked!"

The Book of Morcia was a magical book. It could tell the king about events in the kingdom.

"Who would do such a thing?" asked Sir Santis. "Morcia has no enemies."

"We have one," said the king. "Vladek has returned! His army of Shadow Knights has built him a mighty fortress. In five days' time, he will have the power to conquer Morcia."

"We've stopped Vladek before," said Sir Jayko, the youngest of the knights. "We'll do it again!" The other knights nodded.

King Mathias held up a circular stone. "The Heart of the Shield will help you."

The Heart glowed with magic. "The Heart has given you new and more powerful armor, swords, and shields," said the king. "Each of you already has incredible skills. Now they will be greater still."

Chapter 2
An Unusual Plan

The border was guarded by hundreds of Shadow Knights with fireball-throwing catapults.

"We'll never get past them," said Sir Santis.

Sir Rascus climbed a tree to look for a way around the Shadow Knights, but there wasn't one. "I think it's time for one of Sir Danju's plans," he said.

"I do have a plan," Sir Danju said. He looked at Sir Rascus. "And you're the star."

The Shadow Knights guarding the wagon were surprised when a strange knight approached them, and began doing circus tricks.

"I'll bet you've never seen a Knight of Morcia do this before!" said Sir Rascus.

The Shadow Knights drew their swords. "Get him!" they shouted.

But before they could move, something heavy fell on them. They were trapped inside a barrel.

Sir Santis jumped down from the roof of the wagon. "Good job distracting them, Sir Rascus," he said. "I guess your tricks really are useful sometimes."

"And your strength is handy for throwing barrels, too," Rascus said. "So what are we going to do with this battle wagon?"

Chapter 3
A Terrible Turn

Hidden in the battle wagon, the knights entered the Kingdom of Ankora.

"No wonder they call this place The Lost Kingdom," Sir Rascus said as he looked at the gray landscape. "Who would ever want to find it?"

Sir Santis noticed Jayko drawing on a piece of paper. "What's that?" he asked.

"I'm drawing a map," said Jayko. "The king can use it to follow us to the Dark Fortress."

"That's smart thinking," Santis said.

"Actually, it was Danju's idea," replied Jayko.

Fshhak! A ball of fire flew over the wagon.

"We're under attack!" Danju shouted. "There's a group of Shadow Knights right behind us!"

"Jump to safety!" Sir Danju told the others. "I'll stay in the wagon and lead them away. Whatever

happens to me, you must find the Dark Fortress!"

As the other knights escaped, they saw the Shadow Knights surround the battle wagon. Sir Danju had been captured.

Chapter 4
A Hard Decision

Sir Jayko and the others finally reached Vladek's Dark Fortress. A deep moat surrounded its black towers, and at the top of the tallest tower was a giant mask.

"Tomorrow is our last chance to save Morcia," said Sir Santis. "We must find a way inside."

Sir Jayko was thinking. "We must get into the fortress," he said. "We have to save Sir Danju. There must be a way to do both."

He raised his arm and a golden hawk flew down from the sky. "Carry this to King Mathias," he said, giving it the map he had drawn.

"Sir Rascus and Sir Santis, you must lower the drawbridge," Jayko said. "I'm going to rescue Sir Danju!"

Chapter 5
A Secret Revealed

Sir Danju was locked in a cage hanging high above a river of hot lava.

"Welcome to the Scorpion Prison Cave, Sir Danju," said a familiar voice.

"Vladek!" said Sir Danju. The evil knight's armor was new, but he would have recognized that voice anywhere.

"It's Lord Vladek now," Vladek replied. He held up a piece of metal. "Do you know what this is?" he asked. "It's a fragment of the Shield of Ages. I have already used the rest to make a mask of dark magic.

When I add this last piece, I will have the power to take over Morcia."

Lord Vladek pulled a lever and Danju felt the cage begin to shake. "But you won't be around to see it," the dark knight said as he left. "Very soon, your cage will open and you'll fall into the lava below. Farewell, Sir Danju the Wise!"

Chapter 6
A Friend in Need

"None may pass!" roared the Shadow Knight. The giant scorpion he rode lashed its stinger-tipped tail and snapped its fierce claws.

Jayko had followed the wagon's tracks to the gate of the Scorpion Prison Cave. Jayko had to get inside. The king had said his new armor would make him even faster than before. It was time to try it out.

Meanwhile, the bottom of Sir Danju's cage had almost completely opened. "I guess this is it," he thought. "I just hope that Jayko and the others can save Morcia."

C-RD9-74568-3

As he began to fall, a hand grabbed his arm. "You weren't thinking of leaving, were you, Sir Danju?" asked Jayko, pulling him to safety.

Far below, Danju could see the giant black scorpion struggling behind the prison gate. "How did you get past the guard?" he asked Jayko.

"I ran as fast as I could and got the scorpion to follow me through the gate," Jayko said. "The guard didn't notice that I had cut the gate's rope with my sword. Now they're trapped on the other side!"

"A good plan," said Sir Danju. "But our mission isn't over yet. I know the secret of Vladek's power. We have to get to the Dark Fortress!"

Chapter 7
A Feat of Strength

"Onward!" commanded King Mathias.

He could see the Dark Fortress ahead. Its walls were protected by catapults and Shadow Knights, but worst of all, the drawbridge was still raised!

Inside the fortress, Sir Rascus and Sir Santis were fighting for their lives.

Sir Santis blocked a Shadow Knight's axe with his shield. "The drawbridge is chained up," he said to Sir Rascus. "You've got to keep them busy while I break it down!"

Santis put his hands against the drawbridge

and pushed with all of his strength. The chains creaked and broke with a clatter. The drawbridge came crashing down.

"Well done!" said someone on the other side. It was Sir Danju!

"Where are Jayko and the king?" asked Santis. Danju pointed to the tower above them.

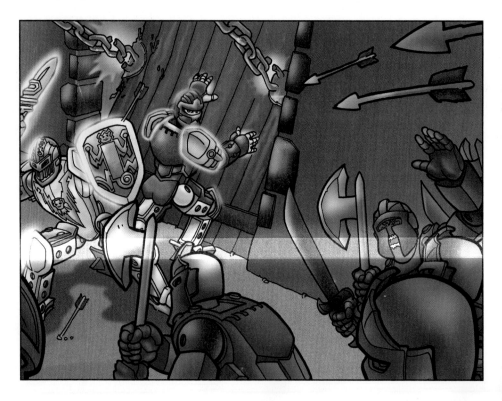

Chapter 8
A Hero's Choice

Lord Vladek pushed the final piece of the mask into place. The mask began to glow brighter.

"Nothing can stop me now!" He laughed. "Morcia will fall before me!"

Atop the tower, Sir Jayko and King Mathias fought side by side. The Shadow Knights could not defeat them.

"I will deal with the king myself!" Lord Vladek yelled, swinging his sword at the king.

"Run, Your Majesty!" Jayko said. "I'll handle Vladek!"

"So we meet again, Sir Jayko," Lord Vladek hissed. "This time I control the power of the Shield of Ages. Do you really think you can defeat me?"

"I must!" Jayko said. "For all of Morcia!"

"Sir Jayko, take this!" King Mathias threw

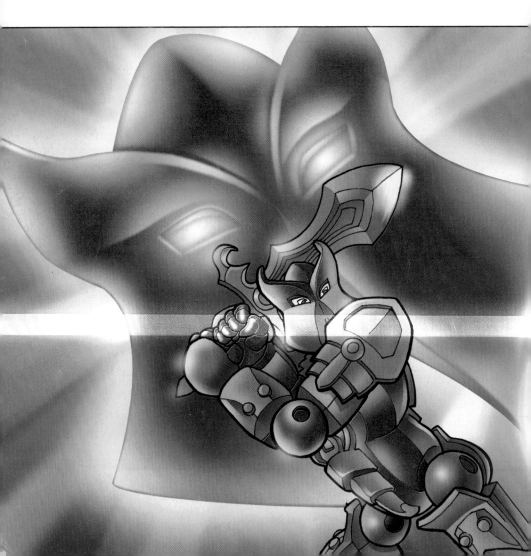

something to the knight. It was the Heart of the
Shield.

Now Jayko and Vladek were both protected by
magic. They fought fiercely. Then Sir Jayko saw his
chance. He raised his sword, but instead of swinging

it at Vladek, he smashed it into the glowing mask!

The mask cracked, shattering into pieces. With the power of the mask gone, the Dark Fortress began to shake and fall apart.

Chapter 9
A Golden Crown

"People of Morcia!" said King Mathias. "Thanks to the courage and skills of these knights, our kingdom has been saved!

"I have had my final adventure," the king continued, "and now I think it is time for me to retire. But your new king has proven himself a true knight and hero. I know that he will rule Morcia well."

Mathias removed his golden crown and placed it on the head of the young knight who kneeled before him. "Rise, King Jayko!" he said.

Jayko stood up. Now more than ever, it was

his duty to protect Morcia and all of her people. Fortunately, he had three great friends who would always be there to help him.

Danju, Santis, and Rascus joined in the cheering and shouted: "Long live King Jayko!"